KHAEMWESET, IN THE UPPER KINGDOM OF EGYPT
huff
huff
dnk
dnk
dnk
BROTHER! WHAT BRINGS YOU HERE SO LATE?
RA-MEI. MAY I COME IN?
I0714504

OF COURSE!
THANK YOU.
IS SOMETHING WRONG, AMEN?
UH, YE
I NEED YOUR ADVICE, RA-MEI.
ABSOLUTELY. NOW, WHAT IS IT?
IT'S... WELL, IT IS A LITTLE AWKWARD TO EXPLAIN.
I AM SEEING SOMEONE.

ONGRATULATIONS!
WHAT'S HER NAME?
DO I KNOW HER?
HIS NAME
IS SEBEK.
HIS NAME...
WHAT?
HIS NAME
IS SEBEK.
HA
HA
HA
HA
HA
HA

HA
HA
HA
HA
I DON'T SEE WHAT'S SO FUNNY—
MY LITTLE BROTHER, THE BIG, MASCULINE BULL, LIKES IT UP HIS REAR!
MAY A DONKEY FUCK YOUR ASS!
NO I DO NOT!
I'M SORRY RA-MEI. IT'S SO COMPLICATED.
PERHAPS YOU SHOULD START AT THE BEGINNING?

WE MET WHEN WE COLLABORATED ON A PIECE MEANT FOR THE PHARAOH'S DAUGHTER.
HE DESIGNED IT, I CREATED IT.
AS WE WORKED WE BOTH FELT THE ATTRACTION, LIKE THE PULL OF THE RIVER'S CURRENT.
AND SOON WE WERE MATING EVERY NIGHT.
THEN YESTERDAY...
AMEN, CAN I ASK YOU SOMETHING?
HUFF OF COURSE. ANYTHING.
NEXT TIME... WOULD YOU LET ME BREED YOU?

UHHH...
YOU NEVER HAVE. I UNDERSTAND.
I CAN MAKE YOU FEEL SO GOOD.
DO YOU TRUST ME?
AND SO I AGREED.
SO? WAS HE GENTLE? HEH.
NO-
MY CONDOLENCES.
NO, I MEAN - I...

I DIDN'T LET HIM.
I'M SORRY. PLEASE CONTINUE.
THE NIGHT CAME. TONIGHT. I WAS NERVOUS, BUT I THOUGHT I WAS READY.
HELLO?
IN HERE!
YOU'RE LATE!
!
!

GET OVER HERE. YOU'RE MINE TONIGHT!
UHH?!
SHWFF
WHAT ARE YOU DOING?
SHUT UP COW, I'LL SHOW YOU!
NOW WHY ISN'T THIS HARD?
I THOUGHT I WAS ON BOTTOM—
SHH!
THUD
SQUEEZE

TONIGHT YOU DO WHAT I SAY, WHEN I SAY...
AND YOU'LL LIKE IT!
GET OFF ME!
WHAT ARE YOU DOING?!
WHAT DO YOU MEAN, I WAS JUST—
YANK
I DON'T DERSTAND.
NO, PLEASE—

DON'T
LEAVE!

OH NO!

THIS IS... A LOT TO TAKE IN.
I'M SORRY TO BRING THIS ON YOU.
DON'T BE AN IDIOT. I JUST MEANT—
WELL, HOW WERE YOU, WITH HIM?
WHAT DO YOU MEAN?
DID YOU... DOMINATE HIM LIKE THAT?

I- NO. RA-MEI YOU KNOW ME.

YES I KNOW MY COCK IS GOING UP HIS BUTT AND THAT COULD HURT IF I'M NOT GENTLE.

WELL I DON'T KNOW WHAT YOU'RE LIKE WHEN YOU'RE MATING!

THE ONLY TIME I'M ROUGH IS AT THE FORGE WITH MY HAMMER.

NOT ONE 'TAKE IT YOU BITCH' AS YOU PLOWED AWAY?

hump

ALL RIGHT, FINE, YES, A COUPLE OF TIMES!

ARE YOU CERTAIN THIS ISN'T JUST ABOUT HOW HE... APPROACHED THAT?

WHAT?

DOES THE IDEA OF SUBMITTING TO HIM, LETTING HIM DO THAT, BOTHER YOU?

I...

WELL, DOES HE LIKE IT? WHEN YOU FUCK HIM?
HE... HE SOUNDS LIKE HE DOES, YES.
AND YOU'VE ALWAYS LIKED MALES, BUT NEVER IMAGINED BEING THE ONE UNDERNEATH?
...MAYBE I HAVE.
BUT IF HE WAS GOING TO BE THAT AGGRESSIVE JUST DURING FOREPLAY,
IMAGINE WHAT HE WOULD HAVE DONE TO ME IF I HAD STAYED!
IT'S ONLY FAIR LITTLE BROTHER. YOU FUCK HIM, HE FUCKS YOU.
BUT MAYBE... MAYBE YOU JUST NEED TO TALK TO HIM.

DO YOU LOVE HIM?
I THOUGHT I DID. YES, I DO.
SEX ISN'T JUST GRUNTS AND SWEAT, AMEN.
YOU'VE ALWAYS BEEN THE SHY ONE— BUT YOU HAVE TO SPEAK ALOUD WHAT YOU NEED.
"SO GO TO HIM. NOW."
"DON'T LET THE EYE OF THE MORNING SEE YOU OUTSIDE OF YOUR LOVER'S HOUSE WHEN HIS SHIP CROSSES INTO THE DAY."
NOD

KNOCK
KNOCK
OH.
...MAY I COME IN, SEBEK?
INSIDE...
I...
I'M SORRY!

I'M SO SORRY! I WAS PLAYING A GAME, A PART. I DIDN'T MEAN TO DRIVE YOU AWAY!
I NEVER WANTED TO HURT YOU — IT WAS JUST TOO MUCH FOR ME.
I OVERDID IT A BIT.
I KNOW. I—
PERHAPS LATER, WHEN YOU MOVE IN AND OUT OF ME EASILY, WE CAN PLAY THE DOMINANT GAME.
SHFF
BUT TONIGHT...

TONIGHT, I NEED THE WORD IN YOUR EYES THAT YOU'LL TREAT ME GENTLY.
MORE GENTLY THAN I PROBABLY TREATED YOU, HEH.
ANYTHING NOT TO LOSE YOU AGAIN.
I SWEAR TO YOU I'LL SPEAK TRUE.
MOOO
NOW, IS THIS BETTER?
OH YES.
slk

hmmf
slrp
hah
hmm
OH.
slk
THIS IS THE
VIEW I WANT
EVERY DAY.

BE CAREFUL
THE PROMISES
YOU MAKE!
I MEAN IT
SINCERELY!
THEN I PROMISE
TO BE THE BEST
YOU'LL EVER HAVE.
OH!
slrp
MMNG!

?!
spurt
MAH
ARE YOU READY FOR ME?

AGH... WHAT? WHY DID YOU STOP?
WHEN THERE'S A COCK INSIDE YOU, IT FEELS LIKE SOMEONE PLEASURING YOUR OWN FLESH, BUT FROM WITHIN.
rustle rustle

shlp

I KNOW YOU NEED REST AFTER YOU COME, SO I STOPPED TO LET YOUR CLIMAX FALL BEFORE WE BEGIN.
I DIDN'T KNOW THAT.
DOES THAT MEAN YOU'RE EXCITED NOW?
PERHAPS MORE THAN BEFORE.
HOW... SHOULD I B FOR YOU?
slk
slk

JUST SPREAD YOUR LEGS A BIT AND I'LL DO THE REST.
ALL RIGHT.
IS THIS GOOD?
OH YES.
THANK YOU FOR COMING BACK TO ME.
WHAT ARE YOU
DOOOHHEMMM?

HAH
OHH
SLURP
ah!
rub   rub
NNNG!
SHLP
ARE YOU ALL RIGHT?
HAHH. YES. JUST STRANGE!

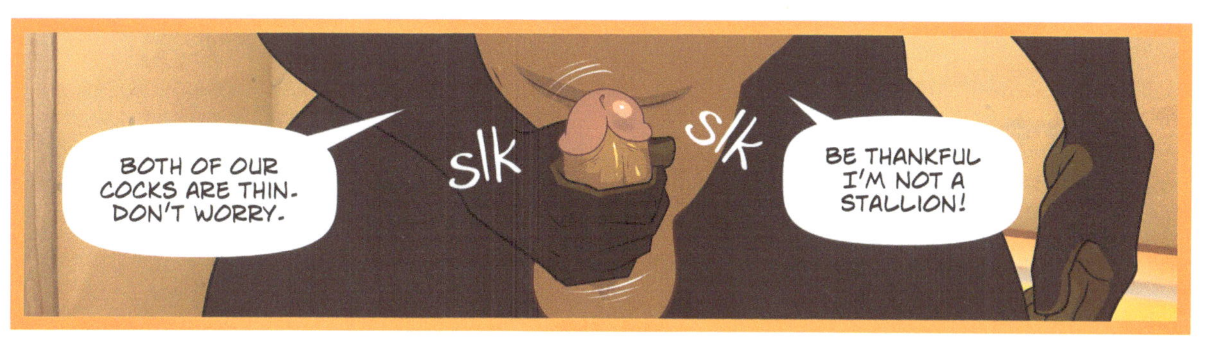

BOTH OF OUR COCKS ARE THIN. DON'T WORRY.
slk
slk
BE THANKFUL I'M NOT A STALLION!

nudge

GRUNT THERE IT IS.

shlp!

ffp

OH...
MY...

HEH. YOU'RE
TIGHT.

YOU'RE
LONG!

JUST A
LITTLE...

THERE. ALL
THE WAY IN.
HUFF THAT—
IS A CURIOUS
FEELING.

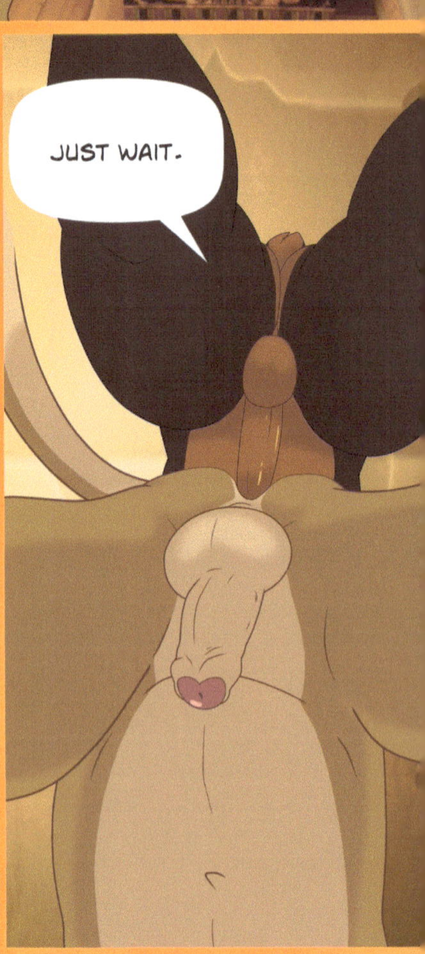
JUST WAIT.

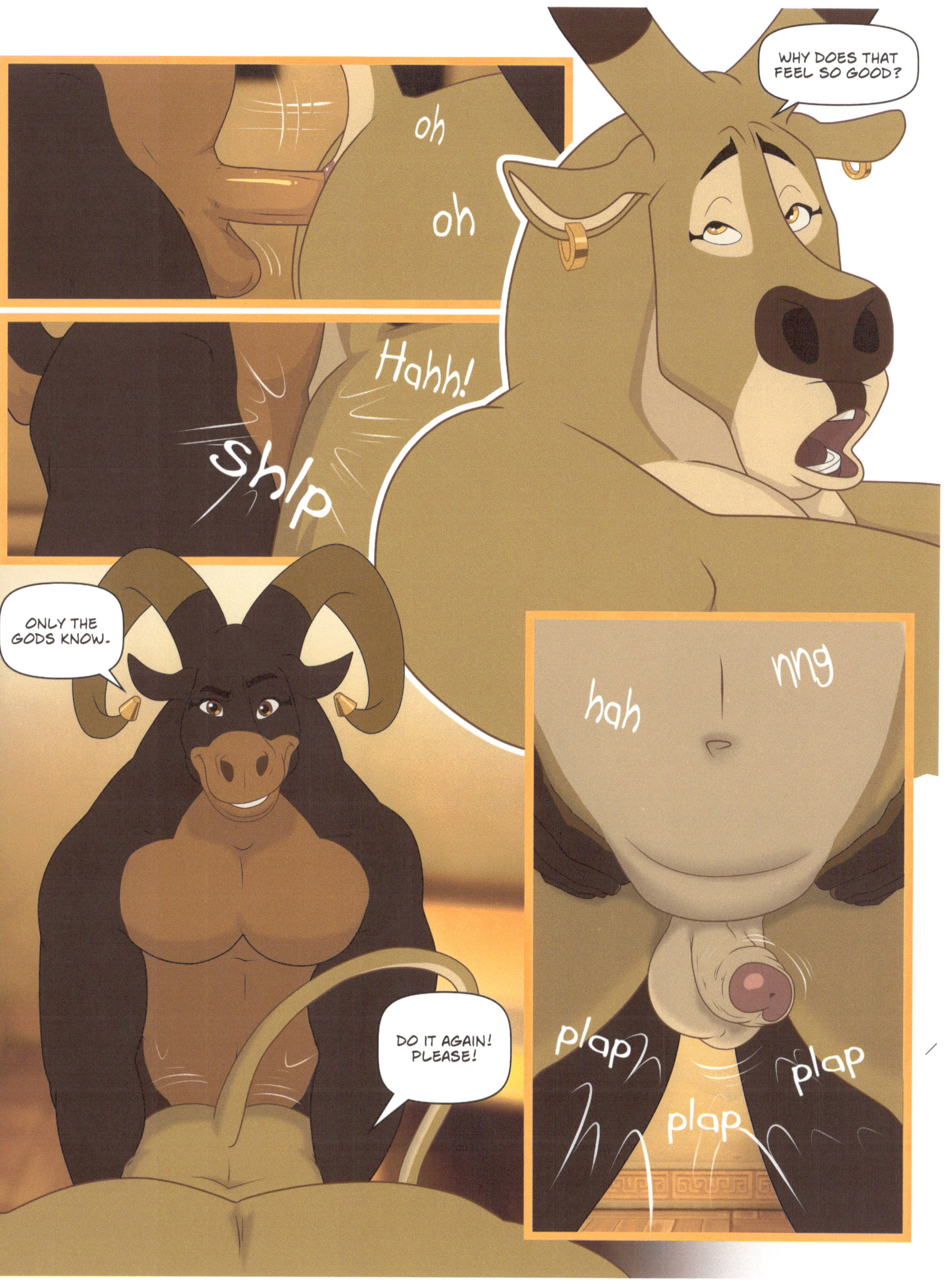

WHY DOES THAT FEEL SO GOOD?
oh
oh
Hahh!
shlp
ONLY THE GODS KNOW.
DO IT AGAIN! PLEASE!
hah
nng
plap
plap
plap

splurt
AAHHH!
OH - OH- I'M-?!
I MADE YOU COME?!
UNHH!
I'LL LET YOU REST-
NO! MORE! GIVE ME MORE!

FFP
PLP
SHLP
PLAP
FFP
PLAP
SHP
FFP
hah
nng
hmm!
mmmng!
shlp

OHH!
CLAP
FFP
PLAP

THAT- THAT'S TOUCHING SOMETHING-
FUCK ME... OOGH.
I KNOW.
SHLP
PLP
FFP
CLP
SHLP
PLAP

OHHHNNG!
HOW ARE YOU MANAGING THAT?
PLAP
SHLP
PLAP
Splt
I LOVE- THIS-

I LOVE—
YOU.
I'M CLOSE. CAN I FINISH?
SLAP
SLAP
SLAP
DO IT!! UGH!!!
OH! NNG!

AHHH
HAH
HAH
HOOH

DID YOU MEAN WHAT YOU SAID? OR DID MY COCK STEAL YOUR TONGUE'S WILL?
WHAT DID I SAY?
I COULD NEVER SAY THOSE WORDS UNKNOWINGLY, SEBEK.
HEH
HAH
THAT YOU LOVE ME.
THEN, I LOVE YOU TOO AMENHOTEP.

THE NEXT MORNING...
HEY LITTLE BROTHER!! HOW WAS YOUR NIIIIIGHT?!

OOF!

SO? HOW WAS IT?
PLAP
PLAP

DOES THIS...
ANSWER...
YOUR QUESTION?
FFP
PLAP
PLAP
FP
SHLP

OH HELLO!
I'D INVITE YOU IN, BUT
I'M A BIT BUSY WITH
YOUR BROTHER'S RUM
COME BACK LATER?

HA
HA
HA
HA
HA

I DEFINITELY WILL! HAVE FUN!

LATER

SO, DOES HE MOO WHEN YOU SHOVE IT IN?

PPFFPT!